BROTHERS
OF THE ZODIAC

AIR

MAXWELL THOMAS

Cover design © 2019 by Niki Lenhart
nikilen-designs.com

Published by Zarra Knightley Publishing
zarraknightleypublishing.com

ISBN 978-1-946907-43-1 (Trade Paperback)

10 9 8 7 6 5 4 3 2

FIRST EDITION

PROLOGUE

PHILADELPHIA, PENNSYLVANIA
PRESENT DAY

I

S CORPIO LOOKED ABOUT FIFTY YEARS OLDER NOW. His partner had died a few months back. Although he would never admit it to his new young lover, he missed him.

When he had received the mysterious text on his phone a couple of days ago, he almost ignored it as a practical joke. But his latent curiosity had gotten the better of him.

"Come to Philadelphia on June 23."

Now he was here, in the airport, not knowing where to go or what to do next. He had packed for an overnight, so had no baggage, but waited in Baggage Claim for no other reason than to people-watch.

Then he heard phones go off in unison. Beeps, bells, and hums. Four men in unison looked down at their phones, but he heard Siri say in his ear, "Go to Pearl's for six p.m."

He looked around and caught the eye of one man, who was looking at another, who stared at a third. Then they all started to congregate toward each other. He knew what they were.

They were Brothers.

2

Now four men gathered in the middle of baggage claim, and others were heading their way. Scorpio joined the cluster of men, who introduced themselves.

"I'm Gemini," said a man with Harry Potter glasses. To Scorpio, he like an accountant.

"We go by that?" asked another man, looking disgusted.

"It's easier," said Scorpio, leaning on his walking cane. "We know who we are."

"Who are you?"

"Scorpio," he said. Man, he wanted a cigarette.

"Well, then, I'm Virgo."

Scorpio studied the ruddy-faced man. Other men gathered until, of course, there were twelve. Some held carry-ons. Some had the clothes on their backs. All of them looked confused at meeting each other here.

Suddenly, a voice from his Bluetooth earpiece said, "Go to Pearl's at sic p.m."

Everyone else looked down at their phones. Scorpio watched as a couple of them frowned.

"What's Pearl's?" asked a redhead with a Scottish accent. Scorpio guessed that he was Aries.

"A bar," said Gemini.

"Why do we need to go to a bar for?"

"I guess we find out," said a man with long blond hair who looked like a surfer. He didn't have a carry-on or any baggage.

"I don't even like bars," said a young man.

Scorpio put his arm around his shoulders. "You just might like it."

3

After further introductions on the way to a rental car, Capricorn had the bright idea to rent a large limo that could seat all twelve. Since even Scorpio didn't have that kind of money, nobody said otherwise.

Hell, if he was paying ...

Sagittarius suggested they go get something to eat.

"Wendy's?" asked Virgo, pulling out his wallet.

"I know a better place," said Gemini.

"Have you been here before?" asked Libra.

"It's been a few years, but I still know my way around."

Gemini pulled down the window between himself and the driver and told him to go to a place with a Japanese sounding name. Virgo wouldn't be able to touch anything on the menu there, except maybe the miso soup.

Aries, the redheaded man with the clothes on his back, said, "Someone's going to have to cover me."

"I got this," said Capricorn. "I have an expense account."

"Rich man," said Leo.

"Most days."

When they got to the place, all of them piled out of the car and looked up at the Japanese icons over the door. Gemini led the way, with Capricorn confidently going in second. Pisces was undecided, so Scorpio guided him in.

Gemini spoke to the *maître d'* in Japanese. The man escorted the group to a room in the back of the restaurant. He slid open the teak and onionskin panels to expose an airy, well-lit room with cushions and low tables on the floor.

Everyone took off their shoes, except Leo — the surfer wore sandals. Scorpio could tell by the type of socks that every man wore whether they were rich or poor. Sagittarius wore mismatched white socks, and didn't seem to care.

As they settled in, two waiters came in with pitchers of water and began to serve them. Gemini perused the menu while Capricorn said, "Just order one of everything."

Pisces turned to Scorpio. "I don't like Japanese."

"You'll love the teriyaki."

"I'm vegan."

Leo said, "Then you're shit outta luck."

"That's not necessarily true," said Cancer.

Leo huffed and drank his water.

Finally, Aquarius spoke. He had been silent the entire time in the airport, the ride down, and had not introduced himself.

"Why are we here?"

The men looked at each other. Scorpio sipped his water.

"The end of the world," he said, while putting down the glass.

Everyone turned to him. "Do you know something we don't know?"

"Today, I'm mortal. I found my true love years ago. Now he's dead." Scorpio shrugged. "I have nothing to live for."

"That doesn't mean the rest of us won't live on," said Cancer. "Whenever one of us dies, another man from Erishkigal takes his place."

"What if there are no souls left?"

"Say what?" Leo almost spat out his water.

"You're just saying that to get a rise out of people," Sagittarius said.

"I believe it, my good friend," said Scorpio with a grin, knowing that he and Sagittarius had often been at odds.

"You're not the center of the universe," said Aries.

"And you are?"

"I'm first. I've always been first."

"First on the calendar, big whoop."

Aries got up. "You've always been an asshole, even though you're old."

"Sit down," commanded Capricorn.

Taurus coughed. "Aries, calm down."

"Easy for you all to say."

Pisces said, "What if he's right?"

"He's not right," said Cancer. "He's just being egotistical."

"Egotistical is not my nature," Scorpio retorted.

"But doom and gloom is."

"Gentlemen," said Capricorn. "Please."

Aries plopped down like a chastised child. No one wanted to argue with the old man of the zodiac: Capricorn, ruled by Saturn, the strict father.

Food came. People dug in, even Pisces. There was no more discussion, but Scorpio knew he was right.

4

Gemini took them on a tour of Philadelphia until quarter of six. Most of the men were getting antsy the closer it got to six o'clock. They parked the big behemoth in front of Pearl's — a nondescript, storefront of a bar.

"I don't think it's going to hold us all," Scorpio said.

"Maybe it's bigger on the inside," said Taurus with a grin.

Capricorn tried the door. It opened. "Let's find out."

They went inside. In the front was the coat room; just beyond that was a bar. Beyond that was a dance floor. Nothing was lit. It seemed to Scorpio that, yes, it was bigger on the inside.

When the door to outside closed, it plunged the coatroom area into near inky darkness. But no one moved forward.

A voice came over the loudspeakers above their heads:

He bade her enter the first gate, which he opened wide, and took the large crown off her head: 'Why, O gatekeeper, dost thou remove the large crown off my head?'

Enter, O lady, such are the decrees of Ereshkigal.

The second gate he bade her enter, opening it wide, and removed her earrings.

Scorpio suddenly felt his Bluetooth disappear. He clapped his hand to his ear in shock.

'Why, O gatekeeper, dost thou remove my earrings?

Enter, O lady, for such are the decrees of Ereshkigal.

And so it went. Bits and pieces of clothes disappeared on each man until they all stood naked. Then some of them stepped forward into the bar. Scorpio guided Pisces inside.

The bar remained dim. Most of the men looked uncomfortable naked in the bar.

"Anybody want a drink?" asked Leo, heading to the bar.

"We're not here for that," said Gemini. "We're here for Lady Ishtar."

"Well, where is she?"

"Here," said a voice from the dance floor. A Middle Eastern woman dressed in leathers, long curly black hair flowing down her back, stood in the middle of the dance floor.

"Lady Ishtar," said Aquarius, and went to his knees. The other men stared at him, before they too dropped to their knees.

She smiled, approached them, touched each one on the shoulder, and had them rise. She stood in the middle of them, but looked directly at Scorpio.

"*Al Allul,*" she said, "is right."

"The end of the world?" gasped Cancer.

"Our world. You are no longer needed. Upon seeing my countenance here, you are all mortal."

"Lady," said Gemini, "We will always be needed."

Ishtar turned to Gemini. "Hm?"

"Humankind always needs help from itself."

Capricorn stepped forward. "Do you deny that the world has no need of the guiding hand of the great Lady Ishtar?"

"The world knows me now," she said. "I have worshipers who know my name."

"Is that all we were to you?" asked Pisces. "People who carried your name?"

"Yes," she said.

"Oh, my God, really?" Leo expressed what was going through everyone's mind. "We were being used?"

Ishtar narrowed her eyes. "I am the goddess of love and war, and I can strike you down here."

"Do me the fucking favor," said Leo. "I'm not going to be someone's chattel slave."

She waved a hand, and Leo fell forward. To Scorpio, it looked as if the man's soul had been ripped right out of him.

The other men gasped.

"Wait now, wait," said Gemini. "Lady Ishtar, please."

"We need to continue being your soldiers," said Scorpio.

"You say that, yet you are mortal," said Ishtar to Scorpio.

"Yes, and I know that I am going to die. But the world needs you, and needs us."

Ishtar frowned. "There are enough immortals in the world. Other gods have their avatars and their soldiers. I will not create another immortal."

"So be it, if that is what you decide," said Scorpio inclining his head. "But what if your worshipers forget you?"

"Who will carry your name?" asked Taurus.

Again, she frowned.

"We praise your name, Lady Ishtar," said Libra. "We praise it and we live by it."

She rubbed her chin. "You are the last immortals."

"Thank you," said Capricorn.

"Please," said Gemini, "return our brother Leo to us."

Leo suddenly took a breath and snapped open his eyes. Virgo and Cancer helped him up.

"The hell?"

"Shh," said Cancer.

When they all looked up, Lady Ishtar had disappeared.

"That was close," said Gemini.

"But we're the last ones," said Capricorn.

Scorpio nodded. "We have to make it good."

GEMINI

♊

I

ROBERT TOWNSEND LOOKED ACROSS THE TABLE at the new boarder in the Underhill home. He seemed slightly older than Robert; but then, Robert was older than anyone else in the room, even though his stated age was 25.

He caught Robert's eye. Robert nodded to him as he took a seat.

Mrs. Underhill, a thin and reedy woman, placed a tureen of stew on the table.

Robert turned to the new man. "I'm Robert Townsend."

"Abraham Woodhull."

The two men shook hands like commoners. Robert took the ladle as Mrs. Underhill cut up some bread. Robert poured some of the mysterious stew into his bowl. It contained more liquid than vegetables or meat. The rations were tight because of the soldiers' needs for their winter quarters.

Mrs. Underhill smiled as she went back into the kitchen. Abraham took the ladle. Robert broke the bread into his stew.

"What brings you to Manhattan?" Robert asked.

"Business."

"Your first time here?"

"No, not at all."

"Where are you from?"

"Setauket."

Abraham bent his head and ate the stew. Robert frowned, knowing that was a dismissal of any more questions. *Maybe he wasn't the talking type,* Robert thought. Or maybe he was merely shy.

After eating some of the stew, Abraham took bread, said a quiet prayer and broke it up into the remnants of the stew.

"What about you?" he asked.

"The same. Business."

"Are you from here?"

"No. Oyster Bay." He still seethed at the fact that some Colonel in the British Army was staying in his house, causing him to stay here in Manhattan. Although it was close to "his father's" business, the situation galled him.

Abraham nodded. "I know where that is."

"I don't remember ever seeing you there. I would remember a man like you."

Abraham looked up, blushing. "I said I knew where it was. I didn't say that I went there."

"You should."

Although older-looking, Abraham was oblivious to the flirting that Robert sent his way. His brown hair was tousled just so, and his blue eyes were like the coral of the sea. His body was of average breadth, but with a broad jaw. Robert smiled at Abraham, who bent his head to sop up the rest of the stew.

But he didn't leave, and that was the important part.

Later, Robert sat alone in the parlor when Abraham entered. "I seem to have forgotten my tobacco." He held up a pipe.

"I don't smoke the Devil's Weed," Robert said.

"My apologies, Mr. Townsend."

"For what? We have a mere difference of opinion. Your business here in town ... what is it?"

"I'm looking to buy an interest in a coffee house. I'm in mercantile dry goods, but the Tories here, they take what they need and leave me with next to nothing."

Robert bit his lip.

"Your beliefs are safe with me," said Abraham with a smile. "I will admit to some Whig tendencies."

"As it is in this house."

"I was told."

"Hm." Robert put aside the book he had taken down to read. He was already familiar with its topic: histories by Plutarch. "You searched out this place for what reason?"

"It was reasonably priced."

Robert laughed. "Not the political discourse?"

Abraham waved a hand, dismissing that.

"Or the privacy of the rooms?"

"How private are the rooms?"

Robert rose. "Let us find out."

2

They went up the stairs, Robert leading. Abraham stopped at his room, but Robert beckoned to his own, which was further down the hallway and away from the main bedrooms. Robert smiled as he opened the door for Abraham to enter.

The room was clean and sparse, without any art on the walls, without anything but a men's shaving and combing kit on the dresser with a mirror. There was a bed, a chair with a desk, a wardrobe, and the dresser.

"Sit here," Robert said, pulling the chair out from behind the desk.

Robert sat on the edge of the bed. Abraham sat, drawing his legs together, unsure of what Robert was going to do, but suspecting what would be next.

"So, your business," asked Robert. "What is it, exactly?"

"To see the market fair."

Robert then made his move, and placed his hand on Abraham's knee. "What do you expect to find there?"

Abraham didn't flinch; he didn't move his leg away. He looked up at Robert, who only gave him a smile. Then, slowly, Abraham nodded.

Robert placed both hands on either of Abraham's knees and leaned in. The kiss was tentative, tender, touching. Abraham shook beneath Robert's lips as he kissed Abraham's neck and ear.

"Is this what you expected?" Robert whispered as he continued to nuzzle Abraham's neck.

"No, but it is pleasant," Abraham whispered back.

Robert kissed him again, and the passion had increased. Abraham parted his legs, feeling himself swelling under Robert's touch.

Again, moving slowly so as to not shock Abraham, Robert began divesting the man of his clothes. Unbuttoning three buttons, he exposed the top of Abraham's chest. Abraham was broad and strong-looking, while Robert was trim, but not as well-built as Abraham. He felt Abraham's chest through the shirt.

"Perfect," he murmured, and continued to unbutton the young man's shirt. Abraham didn't stop him.

In fact, when Robert pulled Abraham up out of the chair, he came willingly to the bed. Robert shrugged out of his vest and shirt as well, while Abraham merely watched.

"Is this the first time you've ever done this?" Robert asked gently.

Abraham nodded.

"Then I shall be careful."

"I don't think I —"

"Shh," Robert said, pushing Abraham's shirt off. "Allow me."

He pulled Abraham onto the bed and kissed his chest, slowly making his way to Abraham's hardened nipples. At a flick of the tongue, he got the reaction he wanted from Abraham — a gasp and a moan of pleasure.

Robert smiled. He explored every inch of Abraham's well-built chest and torso with his tongue and his hands, slowly, leisurely, as if he had all the time in the world.

Which he did.

3

Abraham left the bedroom early in the morning. The two men had not gotten below the waistline, which Abraham had half-expected. *Maybe another time,* Robert thought, closing the door to his own room.

He stripped naked, and all he had to do was feel the chill morning air on him, not unlike Robert's touch, and he hardened immediately.

Part of him had wanted to continue, to go further, to see what would happen. Part of him let his imagination wander, how he would feel if Robert was above him, pressing his body down on him, their manhoods rubbing together as they moved together on the bed —

At that thought, he dropped his hand to his own member and stroked himself. He had nothing to catch the white fluid as he released, biting his lip to hold back a scream, but doing nothing to stop his grunt and panting as he lay back on the bed, staring up at the ceiling.

Maybe later tonight. He was going to be here for the week, after all.

4

Robert slept until sunrise, saddened that he had slept alone for three hours. Abraham was indeed a handsome, strong-looking man. He worked on his parents' farm, which explained his size.

He also was a Whig — not unlike Robert himself. Robert knew that the Continentals had a chance to win the war, with help from Britain's mortal enemies — the French. Also, the British didn't seem to be taking this revolt seriously. The British had Long Island, but the Continentals had the rest of the coast.

Abraham's coming to market all the way from the opposite side of Long Island seemed odd, but there must have been some things that his parents wanted. Produce and farm goods would not be one of them.

Robert shaved and dressed, then went to the kitchen area, where he ate breakfast alone. Abraham had already left for the day. Robert hoped he hadn't scared him off.

Robert left the house and went to the dry goods store of Templeton and Stewart which was located at the Holy Ground — the notorious district where women and men plied their bodies for the British Army's shillings.

He knew most of the boys there — and had casually had relations with some them. None struck his fancy quite like Abraham, though. While he worked, he thought of Abraham and hoped that he was safe.

He also wondered what he was *really* doing in New York City.

5

Robert felt sad the morning Abraham left to return home to Setauket. If he didn't have a job, he would have escorted Abraham back to his home. But then what would happen there? They couldn't dare do what they did in Underhill's home, not under the watchful eye of Abraham's parents. Abraham was skittish enough already.

Robert concentrated instead on building up his fortunes in the dry goods game. The Holy Ground had no lack of people looking for food and clothing, and Robert marked up the items to make a profit. He had money to open his own business.

In fact, he was looking at the possibility of partnering in a business venture with other people.

He thought of Abraham daily. He went to bed thinking of the man who could lay next to him, his head on his chest, fingers entwined as they slept. Finally, he could take it no longer.

He wrote a letter to Abraham:

> 22 February '79
>
> Dear Sir,
>
> I hope this letter does find you in as good spirits as you had left us. I am writing to inform you that I have possibly gathered an interest in a property by the Slip near the Ferry. A patron and I are discussing to open a good store in this location. Which will have a room inhabitable. I have also chosen to assist Mr. Rivington in his local coffee-house. Wherein I should make a good fortune, though I do share it.

I am hoping this missive will Spur you to return to NY soon. I have missed our nightly conversations greatly. Please respond with your earliest conveyance to Mr. Amos Underhill. If I locate elsewhere, I shall see Mr. Underhill to verify if a letter is reserved for me.

I remain,

Your Most Humble Servant,

Rbt. Townsend.

Two weeks later, Amos Underhill placed an envelope at Robert's plate before they ate. Robert's heart leapt, knowing who had sent the letter. He calmly put it aside and ate first, and then sat back to leisurely open the letter.

Dearest Sir,

The missive of 22 February was received with much gladness and happy tidings. I am most humbly glad ye have written as I, too, miss our nightly conversations. The weather in Setauket is not conductive to travel. I do hope to visit NY when the buds attend the sun and the first planting is complete.

Until said event, I will convey my missives hence to those who travel much this way to NY as long *as ye wish to remain thence with Mr. Underhill. If you locate elsewhere, I shalt send these letters to ye thence and ye may use them as your conveyance.*

    The visit shall be soon, I doth promise.

I am, Your Servant,

A. Woodhull.

Robert folded the letter and nodded to Amos. He went into the other room and, as he walked up the stairs, Robert held the letter to his chest.

"... *when the buds attend the sun,*" he whispered.

He opened the door to his room and walked directly to the desk. From this point on, he wrote a letter every week. In the meantime, he met with James Rivington.

Rivington published the Royal Gazette, which carried lurid stories of the barbaric Continentals — and he owned a coffee-house. Robert proved his mettle at the coffee-house by making some of the best grog and, with the money he made at his regular job, was able to buy a partnership in the coffee-house. Many of the British soldiers attended the coffee-house, and sometimes had their tabs forgiven — if they could provide stories for Rivington's newspaper.

Robert didn't find Rivington to be attractive in the slightest, so kept his relationship entirely professional. Robert noted some of the British did seem to be of his type, but, again, he didn't find them attractive. He wanted to wait for Abraham.

One morning, he looked up at the trees lining the walkway to his store. He could see buds on the trees.

"Soon, my love," he said, and stopped walking. *My love? Where did that come from?*

In all the years he'd been alive, five times that of Abraham at least, he had not felt love before. Compared to some of his brethren, he was young, inexperienced.

He couldn't love someone this soon. He had many lives to live. He had come from England just forty years before. He had taken the Townsend name of "his father" who lived in Oyster Bay. When "his father" died, he took on the name of his son and moved out of Oyster Bay as soon as he was able.

As he approached his place of employment, a man sat outside on the stoop. He wore a simple traveler's cloak over his clothes and carried a bag on a pole over his shoulder.

"*Hola, Señor.*"

"Er, hello." Robert looked at him sideways. "Can I help you?"

"You are an investor, no?"

"No, I own this warehouse."

"*Muy bueno!*"

The man tucked a hand in the pouch at his waist, and pulled out coins. Gold coins. How he got through the Holy Ground, the worst place on Earth, with his gold intact surprised Robert.

"You need an investor?"

"I —"

The man pressed three coins into Robert's hand. He stood close to him.

"I need a place to put my money, and you're as good as any."

Gone for a moment was the Spanish accent. The man stepped away.

"*Si, Señor?*"

"Wait."

The Spaniard smiled and walked away with a wave, heading north.

Robert stared at the money in his hand. *Was this maybe stolen money?* Who was that man? And why him?

6

After work, Robert went to his second job. Down the street from the warehouse, he walked into the coffee-house that he owned with James Rivington.

And came face to face with the Spaniard.

The Spaniard was joking with a small group of officers, buying them drinks and playing cards. The officers were severely drunk, soon to be passed out, but the Spaniard was laughing with them, jovial even.

Finally, one of the officers slipped from the chair and onto the floor, which caused the whole group of them to laugh uproariously. Robert watched as, one by one, the officers ended up flat on their backs, or on their rears, out cold.

The Spaniard stood up, wove his way through the tables to the end of the bar, where he ordered a coffee from Robert. The Spaniard winked at him.

"So, *Señor*, what did you invest in?"

"Pork," said Robert, giving him the coffee.

"Will you invest in military goods next?"

"I might."

"Do so." The Spaniard sipped the hot brew. "Hm, your friends can't hold their liquor."

"Or maybe you can?"

"What is your strongest concoction?"

Robert slowly grinned. "Grog."

The Spaniard slapped a coin on the table. "Serve me five of them!"

"As you wish," Robert said, taking the coin, and lining up five large mugs of the liquor.

After three mugs, the Spaniard slurred his words. At four, he barely held himself up, and he couldn't seem to reach for the fifth one.

"You're done here," Robert said, taking the last mug and drinking it himself.

The Spaniard muttered something in his native tongue. At least it might have been his own language, because Robert couldn't hear or understand it. He didn't seem like he was ready to relinquish his spot at the bar, however.

"Where are you staying?" Robert asked. "I can bring you there."

"Nowhere," said the Spaniard. "Anywhere."

Well, the man was investing in his warehouse. He might as well set him up there.

"David," he said to the other worker at the bar, "I'm leaving." He walked around the counter to the Spaniard. "Come with me."

"Where are we going?"

"My apartment. You'll get robbed out there in the condition you're in."

The Spaniard let himself be led back through the streets to the warehouse. Unfortunately, he could not stand up on his own, as Robert found out when he rested the man against the wall, while Robert unlocked the door.

Getting him up the stairs was another feat, but Robert was a strong man and carried him most of the way. He poured the man onto his bed and, when he looked at the Spaniard, he had a mischievous gleam in his eye.

The Spaniard took Robert's collar and tore his shirt open. He had another shirt on beneath it, due to the cold, and Robert jerked himself away.

"Start the fire," said the Spaniard, "and then climb into bed with me."

Again, no hint of an accent this time. Robert faced the Spaniard, who grinned at him.

"What makes you think —"

"You are one of the brethren. Lady Ishtar called you."

Robert's eyes widened. "You know? How do you know?"

He chuckled. "You glow. You will see, as you grow older."

He reached up for Robert, and again grabbed him by the collar. The shirt underneath was thin and fragile, as he wore it all the time, and easily tore under the Spaniard's strong grip.

"I have no —"

The Spaniard didn't care as he grappled with Robert, pulling him to his mouth, and he kissed him. Robert let out a noise — more of surprise than pleasure. The Spaniard brushed back Robert's shirts, exposing his chest to the cold air, making his nipples immediately grow hard.

"No, I —" Robert panted. Wasn't this what he wanted?

"*Por que?*"

The Spaniard's hands roamed across his chest, pausing at the nipples. He rubbed his palm against the diamond-hard nubs, making Robert gasp. The Spaniard raised his body up and licked one nipple. Robert, still panting, struggled to keep control, but he was losing it quickly while this man continued to manipulate him.

Robert didn't struggle as the man undid his breeches, then undid his own. The Spaniard pushed down Robert's pants, pushed them off him, so he was naked in the cold air. Robert had goose bumps everywhere from the chill.

The Spaniard rolled to the side with Robert, pinning Robert down to the bed. The Spaniard's cock was large, its head an angry purple. Robert stared wide-eyed as the man stroked himself even larger. Clear liquid leaked copiously from the head onto his fingers.

Then, the Spaniard thrust a finger into Robert's hole. Robert arched his back and bore down on it, clenching from the inside. The Spaniard chuckled, and inserted another finger in, widening him. Robert gasped and writhed, clenching, wanting more.

He wasn't thinking anymore, wanting only this man's member to be deep inside him, to feel the release of the man, to clench around him.

The Spaniard obliged soon enough, thrusting his cock into Robert's hole, spearing him. Robert cried out and reached up for the man, to pull him down for a long, demanding kiss.

Then began the thrusts, the pushes, the pulls. The Spaniard shoved hard into Robert, over and over, relentless. Robert pulled him in with every thrust, as he stroked himself to a higher and higher height. The Spaniard slapped his hand away and took over himself.

Robert almost bounced on the bed, wanting the man to drive deeper, and to stroke faster at the same time. Robert soon passed the point where he knew consciously that he had lost control, and he cried out again, spurting warm white ribbons onto the Spaniard's abdomen.

The Spaniard let him go and concentrated on his own need, which happened soon enough. He growled as he came, collapsing on top of Robert, smearing them both with Robert's seed.

Robert didn't bother putting up the fire, but instead lifted the covers on the bed. After wiping himself down with the remnants of his clothes, he and the Spaniard crawled beneath the blankets, shivering until they fell asleep.

7

Abraham stomped the snow off his boots as he entered the mudroom of the Underhill home. He didn't want to travel in the cold, but it was necessary for his "business" — a business he planned on asking Robert to join him in.

It wouldn't be lucrative; he knew that himself. Pay was sporadic, barely covering expenses. But it was important to the Continentals — especially George Washington himself.

He looked around the familiar rooms, bumping into Mrs. Underhill in the kitchen. He hugged her; she was family, after all.

"Abraham!" she said. "I thought you wouldn't be back until after the thaws."

"I decided to come early. There's a few properties I need to see."

He glanced around, counted the number of bowls out. There were only two.

"Is Robert here?"

"He moved out a month ago," she said. "I know where he is now. He's along the wharf, near the Holy Ground. He owns a warehouse there." She finished seasoning the pot. "I will have Amos give you the direct address."

He knew it was too late to go there now, especially if it was near the Holy Ground, the worst district of cut-purses and whores on the continent — maybe in the entire world. He brought his satchel upstairs.

The next morning, armed with the address of Robert's warehouse, he meandered his way through the area to the ferry. At the ferry, he would count the number of British troops that there seemed to be. He would note the ships, if any: note building of ships, note dispersion of troops. Then he would return to Underhill's house, write a coded letter to the Continental general, which would be delivered by courier to him.

By mid-afternoon, he had finished his rounds and knew what to tell the general. He went to the warehouse address that Amos had provided him.

He rang the bell from outside, hearing it peal inside the place. Abraham heard someone on the other side, and then the door opened.

A man with brown hair and shining brown eyes stood in the doorway.

"*Hola, como estas?*"

"Uh ..."

"You come to invest?"

"No. I'm looking for Robert."

"He is not here."

The man Abraham studied was handsome — in a foreign sort of way. The accent was alluring. *Was Robert..?*

Of course he was.

"Sorry to bother you," Abraham said, and turned from the door.

The man slammed it behind Abraham, who, dejected, walked back to the Underhill's.

The sooner he got the letter off, the sooner he could go home.

8

Robert returned from the coffee-house to find Juan Jesus Gutierrez still in his apartment. It had been two months since the Spaniard came into his life, and he wished the man would just leave.

He wanted someone else. He hadn't heard from Abraham and it was already May. He had sent a letter, but it was never answered. He tried to remember if he sounded desperate in the letter; he didn't think so.

Juan took him in his arms that night. Robert turned away.

"What bothers you?"

"I miss a friend of mine."

"More than a friend?"

Robert sat on the edge of the bed. "Yes. More than a friend."

Juan put his arms around Robert's shoulders and tried to pull him back onto the bed, but Robert resisted.

"Why are you here?"

"Because I have a need to love a man."

"I'm not the lover you need."

"How sure are you of that?"

Robert glared at Juan. "You need to leave."

"Do you need more gold to invest more?"

"More gold? I'm not a whore," Robert snapped. "If you want that, go fifty yards south."

He got up from the bed, pulled on a pair of pants, and stormed down to the warehouse. There was a chair in his office he could sleep in if he had to.

Juan was gone by the end of the night. He tried to give a kiss to Robert, but Robert turned away from him again, refusing to give him even that.

Robert wrote a letter to Abraham. He poured out his love for the man, then stopped writing in the middle of it. He threw the letter on the fire.

The next morning, a Sunday, after having nearly no sleep at all, he went down to the ferry. This would be his biweekly trip out of Manhattan to Oyster Bay to check on his home that had been billeted by the British. He climbed aboard the ferry and looked out at the small crowd that had gathered on the dock.

He did a double-take, convinced he saw Abraham in the crowd. He ran to the edge of the ferry, which had already left the dock and was slowly heading out to sea.

"Abraham!" Robert called out like a crazy man, as he leaned forward over the railing.

One of the ferrymen pulled him back onto the boat. "Are you insane?" the man demanded. "You could have fallen and drowned."

Robert was beside himself. He had to get back there as soon as possible. To hell with his house. That was Abraham back there.

He stayed on the ferry after it docked in Oyster Bay, waiting impatiently for it to go back to Manhattan.

9

Back in Manhattan, Robert almost jumped off the boat onto the dock and ran … No, it wouldn't do to run. He walked briskly, quickly, to Amos Underhill's home.

It was mid-afternoon and raining when he got there. He checked the stable. An extra horse was there. Was it Abraham's?

He went to the front of the house and rang the bell. Amos answered it.

"Good afternoon, Mr. Townsend."

"Afternoon. Is Abraham Woodhull here?"

"Yes, we are in the sitting room."

Amos threw open the door and Robert could see Abraham looking expectantly at it. Upon seeing Robert, he pursed his lips and turned his attention back to the book on his lap.

"You must be cold," said Mrs. Underhill. "Do you want some coffee?"

"Coffee would be good," Robert said absently, staring at Abraham, who glared at his book.

The Underhills looked at the men, then at each other, and then they left the room.

Robert took a seat across from Abraham.

"Abraham."

He lifted the book, licked his fingers, then made a great deal of turning the page.

"Abraham, it's me."

"I can see that," he said.

"I've come looking for you."

Abraham set the book down. "Why?"

"I miss you."

He snorted, lifted the book again.

"What does that mean?"

"How can you miss me with that man you have?"

"What man?"

"The Spanish man."

"He's gone."

"Not enough for you?"

"I was waiting for you."

Again, he snorted.

Mrs. Underhill entered the room with coffee on a tray, then retreated. Robert continued to stare at Abraham.

Finally, Abraham sighed and put down the book.

"Let's talk about this upstairs," Robert said.

"Let's." Abraham shut the book, putting it away.

Robert left the coffee where it was and followed Abraham up the stairs to his room.

Abraham opened the door and let Robert in first. Abraham hadn't even unpacked his saddlebags, as they were still on the bed. Either he was waiting for the rain to stop before leaving, or he had just arrived.

"You were waiting for me?" asked Abraham. "With another man?"

"It was a mistake. He just appeared in my life. He stayed. I kicked him out last night."

Abraham glared at Robert, and then his gaze softened. "I —"

"Abraham," said Robert, approaching the man.

He took a hold of Abraham's chin and lifted it, planting a kiss on those succulent lips. A kiss on his lover — his true love, the love that made him mortal.

Abraham crumpled, pulling on Robert's clothes. Robert divested himself of everything quickly and then helped Abraham out of his clothes as well. They turned down the covers and lay on the bed, both of their bodies crushed against each other.

"I will never let you go," said Robert.

"You'll have to. My business. Unless you want to join me."

"Yes, yes, I'll join you."

"You don't even know what it is."

"I don't care."

Abraham kissed him. "I'm a spy."

Robert paused for only a moment. "Good," he said, and returned the kiss.

AUTHOR'S NOTE

For further information about Abraham Woodhull and Robert Townsend, read *Washington's Spies: The Story of America's First Spy Ring* by Alexander Rose (Bantam, May 2006).

LIBRA

THE INDIAN TERRITORIES
MAY 7, 1879

I

"JUDGE GREYBACK", he called himself, and everyone knew what that meant. The War was thirteen years buried, but old feelings died hard in the Territories. He rode alone in the desert, they said.

I never thought I'd meet the man myself, to tell you the truth. I was elected Sheriff of a sleepy little town in Indian territory that gave firewater to the natives and bullets to the cowboys. How they were used afterward wasn't my concern; just so long as they kept it out of town, and away from people that came to town.

That was all well and good, until the Packards came.

I thought they were a gang, the five men riding abreast into town. They rode right by the bank, by the saloon, over to the country store. I sauntered in that direction, just in case old man Rivers needed me.

Time passed. No one came out of the store for a good long time. I debated whether to go in myself. As soon as I thought about going in, the door opened. Three men stepped out, holding huge bags of flour. They looked at me, I nodded to them, they nodded back.

Another man came out with two saddlebags, and the last one came out with another bag.

"Mind my askin' how you paid for all that?" I asked.

"We got money," said the last man who had exited the building. All four of the other men stared at him.

"You just move here?"

"Yeah," he said. "Twenty miles north of here."

"Are you sure that's safe?"

He walked up to his horse. "We'll find out, won't we?"

"What's your name?" I asked as he climbed on.

"Herbert Packard." He waved his hand to the other men. "We ain't doin' anything wrong, Sheriff."

"Just checking. Newton's quiet. I'd like to keep it that way."

"By God's grace," said Packard, and turned his horse into the road.

"Mormons," said Reverend Don, standing next to me.

"How can you tell?"

"Holier than thou. Throwing the Word of the Lord around like nothing."

"Maybe you'd better go preaching, pastor."

He shrugged. "They don't let out their women."

"Strange. But if they're settling down here, that means they even got kicked out of Ohio territory."

"No reason they should be here."

I turned to Reverend Don. He looked almost angry.

"Maybe I'll take a ride up, introduce myself."

"Both of us."

"Should I bring a gun?"

"No. This is, how do the French call it … reconnaissance."

"Give them a couple of days."

2

I shouldn't have given them that long. That's when Judge Greyback came riding into town.

He came right to the jail where I was drinking coffee spiked with some whiskey to wake up. He pounded on the door.

"Come in, for Chrissake."

He threw open the door; the dust mites filled the light as he came in. His shadow cast over me first, then I focused on him. He was a tall, gray-haired man, with a mustache and well-kept beard. His broad shoulders filled the frame of the doorway. He reminded me of a silver fox, with bright blue eyes that scanned the area around him and missed nothing.

Damn, what a handsome man, I thought.

"You Sheriff Matthews?"

"Yesterday I was. Today I can be that, too."

Not a snort, a chuckle, or a laugh. "I'm Judge Greyback. You might've heard of me."

"Um, yes?"

I stood up so that I wasn't disrespecting him. He seemed the type that didn't like disrespect.

"What can I do for you?"

"I've come to town to see if you have any cases to be heard."

I made a show of turning to look at my empty jail behind him.

"Not today. Though I'm going to see about someone new in town."

"Oh?"

I waved a hand in dismissal. "Mormons. Up north. Got our Reverend in an uproar."

"Mormons are in Ohio."

"That's what I said."

Greyback frowned. "When are you going up to see them?"

"Soon. I'm in no hurry. They're not going anywhere." I sat back down and leaned back in my chair. "Besides, not like they're doing anything illegal around here."

"Yet." Greyback turned from me. "Got rooms for rent?"

"Above the tavern."

"Figures."

I didn't dare tell him about the cat house across the street.

"I can go with you. Maybe they'll give you a cut rate."

He nodded once.

I got up again and went to the door. I locked up the jail, not that there was anyone in it, and led him and his horse to the Golden Goose Tavern in the center of town.

I tipped my hat to the gentle ladies walking by, and to a few of the men with businesses in the town. Mr. King, Mr. Lamb, and Mrs. Hopewell all eyed the stranger who walked with me. He gave curt nods to the men; inclined his head to the ladies.

"Here we are," I announced, parting the doorway into the tavern.

It was still early, but Paco was there, sleeping in the corner, a bottle already empty beside him, and two shot glasses in front of him.

"Sheriff," called Lady White to me from the bar. "You're early. Or late."

"Then I'm on time." I made a broad, sweeping motion. "Lady White, this is Judge Greyback."

"Pleasure, ma'am."

Lady White chuckled. "Not married — widowed, with this wonderful little place in the middle of nowhere as my little patch of heaven. Can I get you boys anything?"

"The judge will be wanting a room. A quiet room."

"For how long?"

Greyback shrugged. "A week."

"Five dollars."

Greyback muttered something about highway robbery and pulled out a silver coin. "Will this do?"

"Confederate money's worthless here."

"It's pure silver."

Finally, I stepped in. "Never you mind. He's my guest."

"Four dollars for you," she said, giving me a sweet smile.

I gave one back to her, and gave her the four dollar bills. "Includes a drink a day," she said.

"I don't drink," Greyback said.

"Well the water here ain't too fine."

"I'll survive."

"Last door on the left upstairs. Quietest room we have."

"And stabling for my horse?"

"Included."

He tipped his hat. "Thank you kindly." He walked past me to the stairs, and clomped up them.

"Silver." She snorted. "Expect me to believe that."

"He's a judge, Lady."

"That don't mean he's not a liar."

I suppose it didn't, but I wanted to trust this man with my life.

3

I went into the tavern just a little before sunset to see the place already starting to pick up. There were no cowboys for miles around. It wasn't herding season, and the train hadn't come this far south yet. So there was nothing for the men to do but drink and screw women at the cat house.

Greyback was eating dinner in the corner where Paco had been. Greyback had his back to the wall and nodded when he saw me come in.

"At least they feed me," he said, holding up a piece of hardtack bread.

"She makes a hearty stew, even if it's with horsemeat," I told him.

He frowned.

"I'm kidding. Mostly."

"You don't seem to take your job seriously, Sheriff."

I sat with my back to the large window and I leaned back, putting my feet up on a chair next to Greyback. "Judge, I don't have anyone around who hates me. You might."

"What makes you think that?"

"You're a judge. You make decisions and then you leave."

The door opened and Reverend Don walked in.

Suddenly, the place went silent. Reverend Don, his long hair whipping around like Jesus' probably did, surveyed the room, catching the eye of every man drinking or playing poker in the corner. Immediately they all started to look sheepish.

Then he saw me, and came right up to me.

"Sheriff, what are you going to do about those Mormons?"

"Reverend, they're not doing any—"

"They're heathens!"

"What do you want me to do?"

"Don't let them back into town. Tell them they're not welcome here. They can go to the town near the river."

"That's too close to Indian country," said Greyback.

At his voice, the Reverend turned his gaze on the judge. Greyback calmly gave it back to him. I watched the two men, waiting to see who would drop first.

Reverend Don dropped his eyes.

Huh, I thought.

But then he glared at me. "Do something."

"I'll go see them tomorrow."

"They might be running from the law," said Greyback. "We'll both go."

Reverend Don cleaved onto that like lice. "Yes, they may be fugitives from justice!"

I rolled my eyes.

"Why else would they be here?" Reverend Don demanded.

"Because the land is cheap?"

Greyback rose. "We will leave at first light."

I groaned.

He glared at me. "Do your job," he snarled at me as he threaded his way between the tables to the stairs.

Reverend Don watched him go. "You could learn something from him."

"Yeah," I said, and ordered a whiskey. A few on an empty stomach would help me sleep.

4

He pounded on the door to the jail before first light. When no one was in the jail house, I slept on the cot in the jail. When someone was, I slept in the chair.

I groaned. I'd had too much whiskey, maybe, because my head pounded each time he hit the door.

"Stop it, for Christ's sake."

He did, as I got up from the cot. I stumbled over to the door and unlocked it from the inside.

Greyback stood, again filling the doorway like he had yesterday.

"Are you ready?"

"No," I said, and walked over to my desk. I pulled out a flask and took a deep drink. It was pure rotgut, but it would clear my head.

I put the flask away and took down my gunbelt from its hanger behind my desk.

"Let me go saddle up Lola and I'll be ready."

"Use the chamberpot while you're at it," he said.

I blinked. "What?"

"You can't get out of those pants otherwise."

"Whaaaat?"

He turned and walked away from the door.

What the hell did that mean?

5

I saddled up Lola, who was a little upset that she didn't get breakfast beforehand. I'd feed her when we got back.

I used the spot in the barn for my morning libations, wondering why Greyback brought that up. What was he talking about?

We left town and leisurely walked the horses northward. At this pace, we'd get there by noon, maybe — though I wasn't sure where the settlement was in relation to our own. I followed the north road, assuming it would be off that somewhere in the valley.

We were silent at first. Then I finally could take it no longer.

"What was that about my pants?"

Greyback stared straight ahead. "You seemed pretty excited to see me."

"What were you looking at —"

Now he turned to me.

"I can tell, Sheriff." He ticked off, "You're unmarried. You live in the jail. I did some asking around. You don't go to the whore house. You hardly drink. And you never have had a woman in all the time you've been here — at least that's according to my source."

Lady White, of course, I thought.

"After," he said, turning back to the road. "When we get back, come to my room."

"I think the jail is more private."

He smiled, spurred the horse faster.

I jumped to catch up with him.

6

The road north skirted the valley. We found the Mormons camped out inside the valley. There was one cabin, but there were four wagons in a general circle. The cabin was directly north, its entrance facing inside the circle.

"I don't see any women," Greyback said.

"Maybe they're in the wagons."

"They're not Muslim. They don't hide their women."

"Muslim?"

He waved a hand. "Never mind."

"Someone sees us." I pointed at the man looking up at us.

"Well, nothing for it."

Greyback started down the hill into the valley. I jumped to catch up with him.

We approached the men, who had gathered in the middle of the circle. The judge paused at the edge of the camp.

"Packard," Greyback said.

"Judge," Herbert replied in greeting, inclining his head.

"I thought I sentenced you to life."

"Found religion," he said. "They let me go."

"With another gang?"

"I swear to God, Judge, I didn't kill no one."

"You were there. You could have stopped it."

Herbert shook his head. "No. No, I couldn't. I done tell you, he was just a nig—"

"It doesn't matter. He was a man."

I looked back and forth between the two men. Then I noted the group of men that had somehow surrounded us.

"I think, Judge, that everything is fine here."

Greyback turned to me. "Do you know this man?"

I motioned to the men who surrounded us. "Judge, we're fine. They're fine. Everything is fine."

Greyback looked around at the men. "Please tell your men to step back."

"Don't," said Herbert. "Leave them alone."

I started to go up the valley. "Sorry we bothered you. Judge?"

Judge Greyback didn't look like he wanted to leave. I was ready to grab the reins and pull him away. I knew when a fight would start and, if the judge pushed things, then it would start. Six men versus two was bad odds.

"Come on," I called. "Judge, come on."

Greyback finally turned and joined me.

"What are you doing?" he demanded when we got out of earshot. "That man murdered another man three years ago."

"I'm surprised you remember," I said.

"It's hard to forget a man who lynched a Negro in Missourah."

"They're not doing anything," I said. "They're starting a —"

"Without any women?"

"Maybe there'll be some mail-order brides."

He snorted.

I rode up beside him and slapped him on the back. "Is that what you're waiting for? The perfect mail-order bride?"

"Might be."

"Is that what we're going to my jail for when we get back?"

He nodded once.

I grinned at him. He didn't seem to notice.

7

I put Lola back in the stable while he continued on to the one at the inn. I gave Lola some warm mash before going back into the jail.

Greyback sat at my desk. "Soooo, want my job?"

He stood up gracefully. "Is it true what I mentioned this morning?"

"What exactly do you want to know is true?"

Greyback walked over to the door and shut it, locking it. I raised an eyebrow. He then turned to me.

In three strides, he was in front of me. He grabbed my head and planted a kiss on my lips, shocking me with his suddenness and his power. He pulled away, and looked down at my shirt.

"Why'd you stop?" I asked him.

"To undress you."

"I can do that myself. But you doing it would probably be more fun."

"Can you take *anything* seriously?"

I laughed and pushed his jacket off his shoulders. He growled and then started unbuttoning my shirt.

"Hold on there, tiger," I said.

But he didn't hear me — or he didn't care. He pushed me backwards, making me stumble back against the bars of the jail. I put my hands on his shoulders as he kissed me, still rough and demanding.

I struggled to get his shirt off — struggling because he moved his body hard against mine. He grabbed my hands with his, pulling my arms up. He held my hands up by the wrists against the bars, baring my chest.

He bent his head and kissed my chest, sucked on my nipples. With his free hand, he removed my dungarees — stepping on them as he pressed his body against my now naked one. I was up and ready for him, wet and throbbing for him. I panted under his next kiss.

He undid his jeans and sprang out to rub against my own cock. I moaned and moved against him, bouncing my cock with his, trying to feel his wetness, thickness, wholly against my cock. He turned me around, still holding my wrists up, and pushed me face-forward into the bars.

He placed his cock against my ass. I pushed back against him, wanted him inside me so badly. It had been over a year since I'd gotten any tail, and I was hungry for it. He spurted something against my ass, getting a grunt out of him.

Did he already shoot?

He rubbed a finger into my ass, driving it slowly, ever so slowly deeper and deeper. I clenched around him, pulling him inside.

Then, his cock followed.

I only let out a breath, not even a cry, because the feeling was so pleasurable. It was what I wanted for so long, and he knew it.

He rocked against me, first slowly, then picking up speed. He thrust deep into me — long, hard, thrusts, plowing me into the bars of the jail, the edge of the smooth iron bar rubbing against my cock.

Then he paused, slowing down, and grabbed my cock with the hand that had held my wrists up. I kept my arms raised, gripping the bars with both hands.

He panted in my ear, his breath tickling the hairs inside my ear.

"I'm waiting for you," he growled. "Waiting for you to shoot all over this floor."

I cast my head back, and then I did as he had just commanded. My belt hit the iron bar with a ding as he thrust into me one final time. Then the warmth, the wetness, the explosion in my ass.

Still panting, he collapsed against me. Lowering my arms, I took his hands and wrapped them across my chest. I laid my head against his shoulder.

That's when we heard the gunshots.

8

Greyback jerked away. Both of us pulled up our pants. I buttoned my shirt; he didn't bother, drawing his gun and running toward the door.

Someone pounded on it. Greyback pulled it open to come face to face with Reverend Don.

"The Mormons!"

"Shooting?"

Greyback went outside, his shirt flapping in the breeze. I followed behind him, my guns drawn as well.

The "Mormons" held a gun to the head of the town clerk's young daughter, Penny. Greyback stood facing the man.

"Wait, wait," I called.

"I can shoot him."

"And they can shoot Penny."

I held my hands out as I walked out into the street.

"Herbert, come on, this is not helping you."

"I'm not going to jail," Herbert said. "None of us are."

"No, none of you are. My jail only holds one, and I sleep in it. Let her go."

"I have to shoot him," Greyback said.

I turned to face him. He aimed at Herbert's head. Greyback bared his teeth in fury.

"Listen, how about we talk about this? Both of you?"

"Shut up, Sheriff," said another man with an accent that sounded like it came from the Deep South.

I turned to face him. When I did, I heard another gunshot. Then another. Then a volley.

"Goddammit," I said. "Stop shooting."

I looked down. My shirt had a red hole in it ... and the red was spreading.

"Son of a bitch."

Greyback came down from the jail house. "You've been shot."

"I know." I fell backwards, into him. I felt dizzy.

"I shot him."

"Penny?"

"She's got away. I killed them all."

"Wha'd you do that for?"

Reverend Don ran over. He put his hand to his mouth.

"Don't just stand there. Get the doctor!" ordered Greyback.

"He's ... I think he's drunk."

"Get him!" both of us yelled.

"Don't close your eyes."

"It's getting cold."

"Don't close your eyes, Sheriff."

"Billy." I smiled up at him. "Call me Billy."

Greyback turned grey in front of me. His voice echoed as if at a distance. "Don't you dare. Don't you dare!"

9

It's cold.

I open my eyes. The world is colored yellow and brown and black.

Greyback — at least I think it's Greyback — but it's him.

Or Is it him? He's bright yellow.

A man is in his arms.

Who is the man on the ground?

I know instinctively who it is. I don't want to see myself there.

I am in the graveyard, watching people toss dirt onto a casket being laid out. Greyback scowls throughout the service.

After that, Greyback packs his room away into his saddlebags and leaves Newtown.

I go with him.

Time passes.

I know it passes because things change suddenly. The Judge grows older. He eventually returns to Newtown, now called Red Valley, and builds a huge house there.

Although he is older, now in his 70's, he is still sprightly. He never took any lovers in all the time I am with him.

He builds up the cemetery, creates a tomb for himself and places another ancient casket beneath it.

In the house, a group of people gather at a large table.

"Come to us, William Matthews."

I am there.

"Knock once if you are here."

I reach out and knock on the table. The people around the table look shocked — everyone except a woman in a shining silver gown.

Greyback is stunned. "Again," he says.

I knock again. I stand in front of him. He cannot see me.

"He is here," says the woman in the silver gown.

Greyback tightens his grip and glows even more than usual. "Has he been here all this time?"

"Yes," says the woman.

But time passes again, and the room fades away.

I am in his bedroom. He is naked before me, and he stands at the foot of the massive bed.

"William," he calls quietly, raising his hands. "Billy."

I caress down his arms. He shivers. But this time, strangely enough, I can feel his skin.

His glow fades and he smiles for the first time in a long time.

"There you are."

He brought a hand down and placed it on my shoulder. I lean forward and kiss him. He returns the kiss, his arms wrapping around me, pressing against me.

"All these years," he says, after breaking the kiss. "I knew."

I can't speak; it's been too long. All I want is to feel him against me, with me, on me ...

He pulls me down onto the bed. I straddle him. He is so warm as I rub along his chest.

"Quickly now," he says huskily. "I don't know how long ..."

I mount him, and his warmth enters me. I can feel his size, his warmth, and I raise myself and lower myself onto him. He rocks his body with my movements, his hands holding mine, helping me lift and lower my body.

"Now," he whispers.

I feel his warmth spread within me. It fills me with a glow, a gentle yellow light, and I look down at him.

He smiles, sits up, and held me.

But there is a black body on the bed.

"Finally," he says. "Finally, I have you."

AQUARIUS

BROOKLYN, NEW YORK
NOVEMBER 9, 1856

I

B RONSON ALCOTT AND HENRY DAVID THOREAU stood outside the bungalow in the chilly afternoon air.

"You knock," said Alcott.

"No, you."

"I say we draw straws."

Thoreau grunted, then knocked, but stepped down so that it looked like Alcott was first.

They waited, looking like they were ready to run away at the first sign of the door opening.

Henry David Thoreau gulped when he heard the latch lift, and watched as the door opened. What would he say to the man that his mentor Ralph Waldo Emerson had said was the greatest poet in America today? How should he react?

His heart beat faster with anticipation.

A woman stood in the doorway. She smiled at the two men.

"Hello," she said.

"Hello," choked out Alcott. "We're looking for Walt."

"Oh, he's not here. But come inside." She backed away from the door, holding it open for them.

Thoreau followed Alcott into the parlor, but, unlike normal people, they didn't stop there. She brought them past the parlor, into the kitchen.

"I'm making dinner. Will you be staying?"

"No," said Alcott, as Thoreau observed the kitchen.

Full of old-fashioned conveniences, such as ladles and pans hanging from the ceiling, cupboards thrown open, a window was open to the brisk air, the oven burning hot.

"No, thank you," Alcott corrected himself.

"Walt is probably out and about with his friends from the firehouse," said the woman.

"Are you his wife?" asked Thoreau, as he entered into the kitchen.

She laughed. "No, of course not. I'm his mother." She winked at them, as if sharing a joke. "He should be back shortly, Please, sit down. Would you like coffee?"

"No," said Alcott again. "No, thank you."

Thoreau, however, did. He wanted to know more about this mysterious man who lived with his mother — not unlike what he was doing himself.

"Walt often has guests," continued the matron. "I often have to entertain them before he comes home." She rolled out some dough. "Are you sure you won't stay?"

"Certain," said Alcott.

Thoreau finally hit him. "Why can't we stay and wait?"

"Henry ..." whined Alcott, looking sideways at the woman, who didn't seem to mind.

Thoreau hooked a chair and plopped himself into it.

"Have you read Walt's book?" asked the mother, as she cut out biscuits.

"I read some of it," said Thoreau.

"I've read it," Alcott butted in as he sat down. It's wonderful in its simplicity and profanity."

"Profanity?" asked the woman, frowning.

"Meant in a wholly positive manner," covered Alcott, blushing.

"My son is not profane,' she stated, setting the biscuits on the baking pan. "He is a good man."

"Of course he is." Thoreau watched Alcott squirm under the gaze of the lady of the house. "I wouldn't mean otherwise. Maybe that was the wrong choice of words?"

"Maybe," said the woman, putting the biscuits in the oven. "Walt's book, though it hasn't sold exceedingly well, is nevertheless an excellent book."

"Have you read it, madam?" asked Thoreau.

"No, but he's told me about it."

"I see," muttered Thoreau.

"Are you sure you would not like some coffee?"

She turned to the kettle, preparing the hot water to pour it over some crushed beans in a mesh filter over a small cup.

"I will, Mrs. Whitman," said Thoreau.

Alcott leaned back in his chair, looking up at the tin ceiling. The woman smiled at him. She poured the hot water over the beans, handing him the cup moments after taking down another cup from the cupboard above her. She settled down across from them.

"Who are you, so that I may let Walt know?"

"Henry David Thoreau," he said, pointing to himself. "That's Bronson Alcott."

"Mr. Alcott, Mr. Thoreau," she said, nodding to each one in turn. "Are you both from the same place?"

"Boston, madam."

"We had a gentleman from Boston earlier this year."

"Mr. Emerson."

"Yes. He sent such a pleasant letter to my son."

"He sent us here," said Alcott.

"Do you have anything from him?"

"No. We are here to give our respects to Mr. Whitman."

She laughed. "Oh, do not call him that. Call him Walt. He will be upset if you call him Mr. Whitman.'"

"We would not dare to assume such familiarity with such an august person," said Alcott, while Thoreau rolled his eyes.

The smell of baking bread filled the room, making Thoreau salivate. He glanced at the oven. He sat close to it, so it burned on his side.

Mrs. Whitman opened the oven, and the smell was intoxicating. The bread was still on the uncooked side, which was just how Thoreau liked it. He reached in and grabbed one of the rolls.

Mrs. Whitman chuckled and closed the door as he bounced the roll on his hands to cool it off before taking a bite. He took a swig of the hot, strong coffee and sat back with a smile. Crumbs tumbled into his beard, but he didn't care. He was starving, cold, and disappointed.

Alcott snorted in disgust at Thoreau's antics. "We really should be leaving."

"Let me finish the coffee, at the very least," said Thoreau.

Alcott got up when Thoreau finished the bread. He plucked on Thoreau's shoulder to get him to stand up.

"We're done here."

Thoreau sighed and got up, the coffee half-finished.

"Come back tomorrow," said Mrs. Whitman. "I'll be sure to keep Walt at home for you when you return."

"We appreciate that," said Alcott, almost dragging Thoreau out. "Thank you for your time."

"You're welcome here any time, gentlemen." She let them out the door.

Alcott took a deep breath, then hit Thoreau on the shoulder. "Are you mad? We would have been entrapped there forever."

"What's wrong with her?"

"'My son is so wonderful.'"

"'Your son is profane.' That was brilliant."

Alcott blushed as Thoreau started to walk away. "Let's find a place to stay. I'm hungry and cold."

2

They walked down the street and found a room for rent nearby. The two men could share a bed. They'd done it before on the way here, so it wasn't that unusual. Thoreau was uninterested in sex for its own sake, and Alcott was engaged to be married.

After the lady of the house showed them the room, and the two men settled in with their overnight bags, Thoreau was itching to get back outside to find something to eat. By this time, though, it was twilight, and Broadway was lit by gas lights.

"How cosmopolitan," commented Alcott.

"It's very nice. Now let's get something to eat."

Alcott took Thoreau's arm and steered him into a doorway. "Here."

Thoreau looked up: *Empire House*. A gentleman left the tavern, holding the door open for them.

"It might be ex—"

"Henry, *carpe diem*."

He sighed, and followed Alcott into the darkened tavern.

The two New Englanders floundered their way inside and sat down at an empty table. A woman quietly served them beer, then left them.

Alcott smiled, sipped the warm beer, and leaned back in his chair. Thoreau perused the paper with the menu, frowning the entire time.

"What's wrong, Henry?"

"It's as I feared — very expensive."

"Oh, Henry, open your purse once in a while."

The woman returned, looking down at the two men.

"Soup," said Thoreau, setting aside the menu.

"Ignore my friend," said Alcott, waving a hand at Thoreau. "He's too frugal for his own good, so I will pay for him."

The woman said nothing, looking for all the world bored and angry.

Alcott took up the menu with a flourish. "We will begin with the conch and capers ..." He proceeded to order rich seafood dishes, three of them, to compare them all against what they were familiar with in Boston.

"Haddock is haddock," said Thoreau. "Besides, I do not eat fish, you know that."

"You eat food for a rabbit. Try something different for once."

"I've had fish. It's disgusting."

"What about conch?"

"It's fish. I will not eat it."

When the dishes arrived, Thoreau stuck to his soup while Alcott gorged himself on all the dishes. He ate two of them, including half of the conch and capers, and just half of the third dish. Thoreau knew his limits. Alcott sat back, holding his stomach.

"Now you will settle down," said Thoreau.

"I want to try the house whiskey."

"I don't think this establishment will have it."

"Then we'll go to one that does!"

Thoreau groaned as Alcott rose, throwing down some money. He shook his head at the waste.

They walked a little more along Broadway, keeping their wallets close to them in case of pick-pockets. Alcott ducked into another tavern. This one smelled of liquor.

He approached the bar and demanded house-brewed whiskey. He got a Kentucky bourbon instead. Thoreau watched as he got three of them.

He drank one, offered one to Thoreau. Thoreau shook his head.

"Have you no want to live?" asked Alcott, as he downed a second shot.

"I don't need to live like this," stated Thoreau. He got some dirty looks from the men at the bar.

"What're you doin' here, then?" demanded one man.

"I'm with him."

"Him" had just had his third and final shot. Alcott turned to Thoreau, his eyes glassy and unfocused. Again, Thoreau sighed.

"He looks ready to leave," said another man, gulping a shot. "Need a little help?"

"I will be fine," said Thoreau, approaching Alcott. "Come now, let us go home."

"We'll help," said a second man.

The first one who spoke him also peeled away from the bar. *Three against two, with one incapacitated,* thought Thoreau.

Two men took a hold of Alcott on either side of him. Alcott swiveled his head slowly, like a confused puppy. Thoreau stepped forward, but another man held him back. The two men near-carried Alcott out the door. Thoreau jumped to follow, noting he was being followed.

The two men took him down the alley. Thoreau dug his heels in saying, "Wait," but the man behind him grabbed him and pushed him into the alley.

One of the two started to pat Alcott down. Thoreau ran forward now. The man behind Thoreau tackled him, slamming him into the cobblestones and the slime of the alley.

Thoreau squirmed, yelling "Help!" as he tried to turn around to face his attacker.

The man was on top of him, feeling for his wallet in his pocket.

"Help!" Thoreau yelled again. "Thief!" He was cuffed on the side of the head.

"Shut up, you fool," the man snarled, getting up, leaving Thoreau on the ground.

Thoreau looked over to see Alcott slumped against the wall, passed out.

The three men laughed and walked away. Luckily, Alcott and Thoreau did not carry all their money on their person, so only the evening's money was gone.

Thoreau hung his head and crawled over to Alcott. At least he wasn't beaten, and Thoreau could stand up. He heaved himself up, using the wall to help him, and waited for the shakes to pass.

He slapped Alcott. Alcott moaned. Thoreau had to pick up the deadweight, which he could, so he put one of Alcott's arms over his shoulders and hoisted him up. He half-carried, half-dragged the man out of the alley to the hotel down the street.

3

The next morning, Thoreau was in a better condition than Alcott. Alcott could not keep anything down and his head pounded.

"That will teach you," Thoreau said, munching on toast with jam.

Alcott held his head up with both hands. "I'm ready to stay here. You go to see Mr. Whitman."

"Alone?"

Alcott slowly rose, swallowed audibly. "He won't do anything to you," he said. "You're a virgin."

Thoreau felt his face get hot. Alcott patted Thoreau's shoulder and headed back upstairs, nearly running there. Thoreau looked around to make sure no one had seen him blush, or heard the statement. No one else was in the room, thank God.

He gathered his coat and, bareheaded, went out into the cold Monday morning. There were more people on the street this time. He wondered, initially, if he was going to arrive too early.

Thoreau stood outside of Whitman's bungalow, and finally got the nerve to knock. He stepped down so that the door could open and Whitman would have to look down at him to see him.

The door opened. A brawny man stood there, wearing a coarse muslin shirt and blue workers' pants, well-worn at the knees. He was barefoot. His hair was longer than Thoreau had seen; but then, this was New York.

He looked across the way, and then down to Thoreau. A smile spread across his features, crinkling up his eyes.

"To whom do I have the pleasure?" the man asked in a voice too high for that brawn.

"Henry David Thoreau. You may have met my patron, Ralph Waldo Emerson."

"Yes, yes, he'd spoken of you. Come inside, come inside, out of the cold."

Thoreau walked up the stairs, hands in his pockets, looking for a moment like a chastised child.

Whitman came up behind him and brushed his hands along Thoreau's shoulders. "Let me take your coat."

Thoreau unbuttoned his coat. Whitman's hand stayed a bit too long on his shoulders, but Thoreau slowly tugged the coat off, hanging it on a coat rack.

Whitman smiled — a generous smile that was welcoming. "Come on up."

"Up?"

But Whitman already went up the set of stairs on the side of the hallway that led to the kitchen. They would lead, he guessed, to the bedrooms. Thoreau stopped at the top of the stairs, almost said something. Whitman smiled, ducked into a room.

Thoreau heard the crackling fire in the fireplace. The window shades were open to the cold November light. The room itself seemed warm — too warm for November. Whitman shut the door to the bedroom and turned to face his guest.

"So you're the hermit."

Thoreau shrugged.

"I've read your work." Whitman sat on the edge of the bed.

"You have?"

Whitman nodded and turned his body sideways, so that he was laying across the bed. He crooked his arm and lay his head on his hand, regarding Thoreau. "You hold a love for Nature like men hold a love for God."

"Nature is the center," said Thoreau. "The center of our being."

"Not God?"

"God is Nature."

"What about love?"

"What about it?"

"Where is that in the scheme of things? You love Nature, but do you love Man who is a part of that Nature?"

"I'd rather be without people if I could."

Whitman's eyes gleamed. "Come now, Henry — may I be so familiar enough as to call you Henry?"

"You may, sir."

"Call me Walt. All my lovers do."

Thoreau flushed red under his beard.

"You do love me, since you are here, yes?"

"Love means different things. I have read your work, also, sir. Walt."

"And?"

"I find it profane."

Whitman laughed, flopping onto his back on the bed. "Ah, you would, my hermit."

"What do you mean by that?"

Whitman turned his head. "Come closer."

Thoreau rose from the winged-back chair and approached Whitman. Whitman gripped Thoreau by the wrist and yanked him to the bed, turning him over onto his back and straddling Thoreau.

Thoreau panted as if the wind had been knocked out of him. Whitman sat on Thoreau's groin, moving slowly against Thoreau's crotch.

"Do you feel nothing, my hermit?"

"You ... sir, are trying to seduce me."

"Am I?" Whitman asked, his eyes shining. He leaned forward and kissed Thoreau.

Thoreau jerked his head back onto the bed. He heard a woman's call from downstairs.

Saved, Thoreau thought.

"Walt, I'm back."

"I have a guest," Whitman returned, with a tilt of his head. He loomed over Thoreau. "She's not really my mother."

"No?"

"No. My mother died a long time ago. As did my brothers, and sisters, and father."

"But the newspaper said you live with your mother."

"As do you?"

"Well, yes."

Whitman laughed again, undoing the tie around Thoreau's neck. "So prim, so proper."

"Sir — Walt — I —"

Slowly, he flicked open the buttons along Thoreau's shirt. Thoreau felt helpless in the strong grip of this man, whose thighs held him down on the bed, whose weight settled on top of him.

Whitman parted open his shirt. "I will let your seed come upon my breast," he said with a husky whisper. "Once, of course, you release."

He tried to kiss Thoreau again, but Thoreau pulled back again.

"No kisses. I understand."

"Walt, this is not —" He grunted when Whitman grabbed his crotch roughly.

"Still not swollen enough? What must I do, be naked for you?"

Thoreau's eyes went wide as Whitman peeled off his shirt.

The man was well-built, Thoreau gave him that — a workman's body, chiseled and rough, with deep lines like Michelangelo's David. Whitman undid his own pants, one leg at a time, pushing the pants — without underclothes — down and letting the pants fall onto the floor.

Whitman was also well-endowed. Thoreau didn't know where he was planning on putting it.

Whitman sighed and stroked himself: long, slow, hypnotic strokes that drew Thoreau's attention.

"Ah, my hermit, you wish to be a voyeur, instead."

He felt Whitman part his pants, to pull out his own member — smaller and more limp than Whitman's, by far. Whitman was not going to leave him alone until he had spent his seed. Thoreau closed his eyes, resigned to his fate.

He placed himself far away, back in Walden Pond. There he remembered a tree, with a moss-covered hole just below his waist. It took come creative maneuvering, but he could get himself into the soft moss of the tree. He felt that, arching his back automatically, moaning aloud.

"There," said Whitman.

But Thoreau didn't let the word invade his memory. He remembered loving that tree: its roots buried deep beneath his feet, and the moss wrapped around his member, the tightness of the unrelenting wood. He panted, joining with Whitman's pants, and then he felt wetness upon his chest.

He felt his rising, and then, it came upon him suddenly: *la petit mort* — a blacking out while he impregnated the tree, like the sky god to the Earth goddess.

He felt someone caress his face. He opened his eyes to see Whitman staring down at him.

"Where did you go?" Whitman asked, concerned.

Thoreau pushed him away, rolling him onto his back.

"I must leave."

He was confused, still shaking from the fit of orgasm. He rebuttoned his shirt, askew by one button, not bothering to tie his tie. He threw open the door as Whitman pulled on his pants.

Thoreau rushed down the hall, the stairs, grabbing his coat as Whitman stood at the top of the stairs wearing his shirt half-tucked.

Thoreau didn't stop running until he got to the hotel.

4

My hermit, my heart, what beauties you have seen
   in woodland day

And night,

The maples with their mighty bows above your head,
   crowning cathedrals of the New England winter,

Roots pitted beneath your moccassined feet,

No boots for you, my hermit,

For you live close to the land, and the land lives
within you, and you show the land the beauties

Of sight.

5

"I've already seen him," said Thoreau. "Once was quite enough."

Alcott tugged Thoreau's arm as they walked down Broadway to Brooklyn. "I don't want to go in alone."

Thoreau imagined the man doing to Alcott the same thing he did to him. Thoreau didn't tell Alcott what had happened between them; he would take it to his grave, and only hoped that Whitman would do the same.

Thoreau sighed and turned his body toward Brooklyn. Alcott smiled and led the way down Broadway to Whitman's apartment. Thoreau wondered fleetingly if Whitman would try to seduce both of them at the same time. The thought sent a cold chill through him.

Alcott and Thoreau arrived soon at the apartment. Alcott nodded to the door. Thoreau walked up the stairs and knocked on the door. Whitman opened it, standing there at the top of the stairs. Thoreau looked up at him.

"I've brought a friend."

"So I see. Please come in."

Alcott held out his hand. "Mr. Whitman, what a delight it is to finally meet you."

Thoreau rolled his eyes as Alcott gushed over Whitman — who smiled and accepted the complements with much good grace. Again, Whitman pulled them upstairs to the bedroom.

"This is the warmest room in the house, you see," said Whitman, as he sat on the edge of the unmade bed. The chamber pot hadn't even been put away.

Alcott continued heaping praise on Whitman, every once in a while turning to Thoreau.

"Isn't that right, Henry?"

Thoreau would only grunt in response.

"Let's go downstairs," said Whitman, standing up. He led the way downstairs to a colder part of the house.

There, Whitman took a standing position while the other two men sat in cold, uncomfortable chairs.

Thoreau wondered why Whitman had done this. A part of him wondered if he was no longer attracted to him.

The lady doth protest too much, he thought.

"We should be a voice for the workers, for the masses," Whitman was stating.

Thoreau found his voice. "The masses don't need a voice if they speak *en masse*."

"They don't speak with one voice."

"So we should speak for them?"

"We should be their voice."

"For whom? To whom?"

"To people like you."

Thoreau's eyes narrowed. "Like me?"

"Elitist."

"Excuse me, sir, but I don't think —"

Alcott grabbed Thoreau's arm. "Henry."

Thoreau hadn't noticed that he had stood up. Whitman leaned against the mantle, smiling as ever, but it was a smile of a man who knew he had poked the wasp's nest — and was happy about stirring it up.

"I think we'd better leave," Alcott said, rising also.

Whitman inclined his head as if to say, *There's the door.*

6

When young Thoreau left with his companion — *His lover or his friend?*, Whitman wondered — Whitman sat down in the chair.

He had hoped Henry would have arrived again by himself. He enjoyed the young man. After seeing him get hot and bothered about the workers, when even manly love didn't seem to arouse him, that made it all the better.

"I should write a poem," he said. "A sniveling, praiseworthy poem, praising myself to the Heavens."

Whitman laughed, the only person in the house. Dorothy had stepped out again, knowing he liked to take gentlemen callers in the morning, and not liking to be in the home when he did.

Instead, he would love another firefighter today. And love many men and boys throughout his long life, even when he knew his end was near.

For now, in this day and age, he could love all men, as he was born to do. He could see the love reflected in each man's eyes.

Even the hermit's.

YOU MIGHT ALSO ENJOY

Earth
A Brothers of the Zodiac Collection
by Maxwell Thomas

Three stories of the Earth signs: Capricorn, Taurus, and Virgo.

Fire
A Brothers of the Zodiac Collection
by Maxwell Thomas

Three stories of the Earth signs: Aries, Leo, and Sagittarius.

Water
A Brothers of the Zodiac Collection
by Maxwell Thomas

Three Stories of the Water signs: Cancer, Pisces, and Scorpio.

Available from Zarra Knightley Publishing
in trade paperback, digital, and audio editions.

zarraknightleypublishing.com

www.ingramcontent.com/pod-product-compliance
Lightning Source LLC
Chambersburg PA
CBHW032110170626
46808CB00008B/3005